The "Baby, Why Do You...?" Series

"Baby, Why Do You Smile in Your Dreams?"

ALISON COLEMAN

WestBow Press books may be ordered through booksellers or by contacting:

WestBow Press
A Division of Thomas Nelson & Zondervan
1663 Liberty Drive
Bloomington, IN 47403
www.westbowpress.com
1 (866) 928-1240

ISBN: 978-1-9736-9180-8 (hc)
ISBN: 978-1-9736-8779-5 (sc)
ISBN: 978-1-9736-8780-1 (e)

Library of Congress Control Number: 2020904944

Print information available on the last page.

WestBow Press rev. date: 05/21/2020

WestBow
PRESS®
A DIVISION OF THOMAS NELSON
& ZONDERVAN

Dedicated to my daughters,
who are my reasons to smile.

My little sister, Sunday, sleeps a lot.
I suppose there are tons of reasons why
my sister gets so sleepy during the day.

"Sunday is a baby, which is why she needs to sleep more than you do, Roxanna," my mommy tells me.

Hhhmmm, maybe?...
But Louie, I wonder what
is making Sunday smile in
her sleep?

Hhhmmm, maybe?...
Maybe Sunday is dreaming about eating a huge chocolate chip cookie which makes her smile?

Mmm! Yummy!
Then afterwards, she is dreaming about drinking a giant bottle of milk to wash the cookie down.

Louie, maybe?...
She is dreaming about riding on a bright
sparkling rainbow flying through the blue sky?

Or maybe?...
Sunday is dreaming about feeding a baby unicorn in a meadow of daisies?

When I asked my mommy again, she told me that Sunday is having a happy dream filled with light.

But I wonder?... Sunday, why does the light make you smile?

James 1:17 NKJV: "Every good gift and every perfect gift is from above, and comes down from the Father of Lights..."

Psalm 127: 3 NLT: "Children are a gift from the Lord; they are a reward from Him."

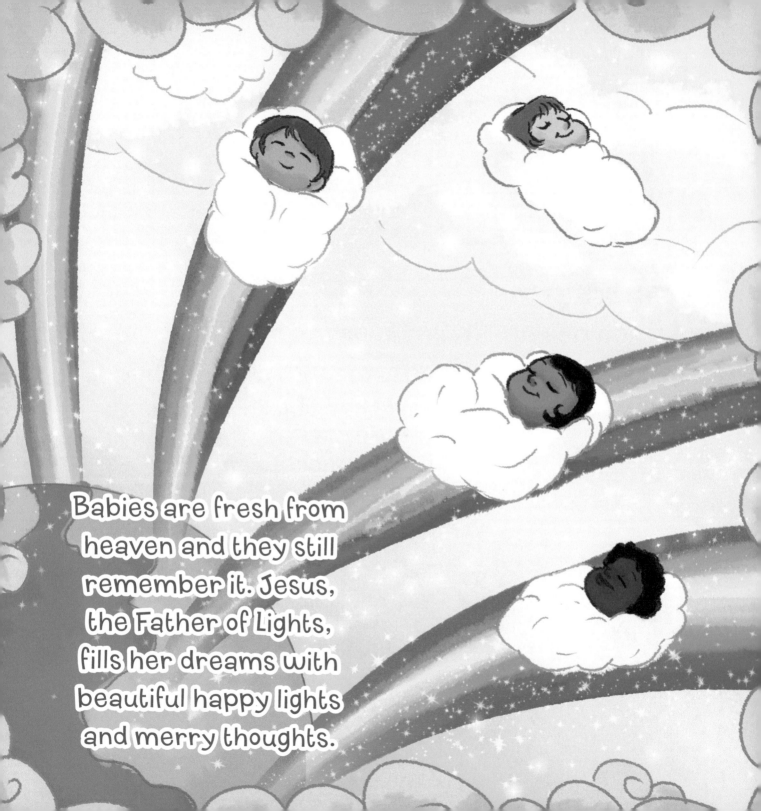

Babies are fresh from heaven and they still remember it. Jesus, the Father of Lights, fills her dreams with beautiful happy lights and merry thoughts.

"Every good gift comes from Jesus" (James 1:17 NKJV).

Louie, she may be smiling about all those good and happy thoughts combined because Jesus gives good things (James 1:17 NKJV). My mommy said, "Roxanna, you and Sunday are my rewards from Jesus (Psalm 127:3 NLT) and you both are my reasons to smile.

Thank You Father of Lights (James 1:17 NKJV), for making Sunday smile during the day and in her dreams too!

Bibliography

New King James Version Bible, James 1:17.
New Living Translation Bible, Psalm 127:3.

Printed in the United States
By Bookmasters